BOOK FOUR

On the Go
with
Mr. and Mrs. Green

KEITH BAKER

Harcourt, Inc.

Orlando   Austin   New York   San Diego   Toronto   London

For Ginger, who understands green

visit us at www.abdopublishing.com

Reinforced library bound edition published in 2008 by Spotlight, a division of ABDO Publishing Group, 8000 West 78th Street, Edina, Minnesota 55439. This edition was published by agreement with Harcourt, Inc. www.harcourt.com

Library of Congress Cataloging-in-Publication Data
This title was previously cataloged with the following information:

Baker, Keith, 1953-
    On the go with Mr. and Mrs. Green / Keith Baker.
    p. cm. " Book Four."
    Summary: Mr. and Mrs. Green, a loving alligator couple, practice magic tricks, bake cookies, and dream up new inventions.
    [1. Magic tricks--Fiction. 2. Cookies--Fiction. 3. Inventions--Fiction. 4. Alligators--Fiction. 5. Humorous stories.] I. Title: On the go with Mr. and Mrs. Green. II. Title.
PZ7.B17427On 2006
[Fic]--dc22

                                        2005002660

All Spotlight books have reinforced library binding
and are manufactured in the United States of America.

Contents

Magic Trick

Mr. Green had a new hobby—magic.

"I need to practice my vanishing trick," he said,

"and I need an assistant."

"Will it be scary?"
asked Mrs. Green.

"A little," he said.
"Okay!" she said.
(Mrs. Green liked
a little scary.)

"First, you'll disappear from this box,"
said Mr. Green.
"Then—faster than you can say 'sassafras'—
I'll bring you back!"
(*Sassafras* was this trick's magic word.)

Mr. Green began.

"Ladies and gentlemen,

look closely—

no secret walls . . .

no secret doors . . .

no secret floors . . .

NO ESCAPE!"

He helped Mrs. Green
into the box.
(She fit perfectly.)

He spun the box around three times.
He tapped it with his magic wand
and said, "*Sassafras!*"

Then he opened the box.

It was empty—entirely empty (except for air).

"Now folks," said Mr. Green,

"time to bring her back!"

(He couldn't *wait* to see her again.)

He spun the box around three times,

tapped it, and said, "Sassafras!"

Oh, dear! thought Mr. Green
when he opened the door.
That's not Mrs. Green.

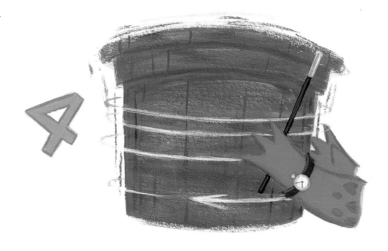

He closed the door and spun
the box around *four* times.

Still no Mrs. Green.

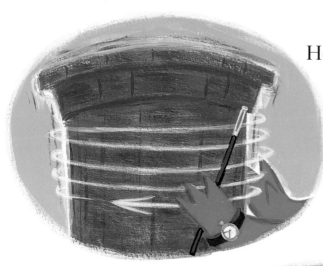

He tried **5** spins,

then **6**

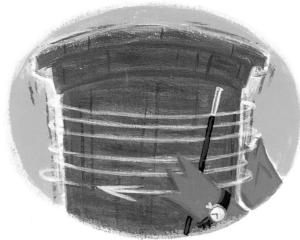

then **7** spins,

14

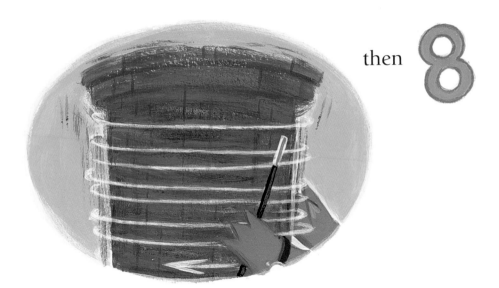

then **8**

all the way to **39** spins.

Still no Mrs. Green (not even close).

Mr. Green took a deep breath
and tried some new magic words.

hocus-pocus!

BOOMERANG!

tutti-
frutti!

spaghetti-o!

Piggly Wiggly!

Walla Walla,
Washington!

But none of them worked.

There was no sign of Mrs. Green.

None at all.

Or was there? Mr. Green saw something pearly,
tick-tocky—a watch! *Mrs. Green's* watch!

He examined it,
searching for a clue.

The second hand ticked
round and round and round,
from 12 to 3 to 6 to 9—
AHA!
The watch gave
Mr. Green
an idea.

He quickly spun the box three times
in the opposite direction—*counter*clockwise.
(Not clockwise as he had before.)

He tapped the box and said, *"Sassafras!"*

Then he slowly opened the door.

(But he closed his eyes—

What if she wasn't there?)

But she was!

"You're back!" said Mr. Green. "I *missed* you!"

"I missed you, too!" said Mrs. Green.

"It was dark and dizzy and scary—
   let's do it again!"

"*Hmmmmm . . . ,*" said Mr. Green,
"what about a *different* magic trick?"
"Will it be scary?" asked Mrs. Green.
"A little."
"Okay!" she said.

"Ladies and gentlemen," said Mr. Green,
"look closely!
No ropes or wires here . . .
no ropes or wires there . . .
no ropes or wires
A N Y W H E R E !"

He tapped Mrs. Green with his magic wand
and said, "Fiddle-Faddle!"
(*Fiddle-faddle* was this trick's magic word.)

Then he slowly raised his arms.

Mrs. Green began to float in the air.

She felt lighter than a lizard,
lighter than a leaf,
lighter than a lullaby.
"This is fun!" she said.
"I don't *ever* want to
come down."

Down, thought Mr. Green.

Oh, dear Houdini . . .

I should have thought of that!

Cookies

Mr. Green woke up from his nap.

He smelled cookies, *freshly baked* cookies.

He followed his nose.

(He had a big nose—it was easy to follow.)

There *were* freshly baked cookies.

And a note. It was from Mrs. Green.

Terrible?

thought Mr. Green.

DO NOT EAT?

He and Mrs. Green had baked *millions* of cookies—
none of them terrible. What was wrong with these?

33

Had Mrs. Green forgotten the butter?

The sugar?

The flour?

The spices?

No . . . Mr. Green could *smell* these things.

Had she forgotten the chocolate chips?

The butterscotch bits?

The peanut pieces?

The miniature marshmallow morsels?

No . . . Mr. Green could *see* these things.

What else could be wrong?

There was only one way to find out.

He took a bite.

Snappity-snap . . .

crunchity-crunch . . .

chewity-chew . . .

deeeeeeeeee-licious!

But were they *all* delicious?

Mrs. Green would want to know.

So he ate another . . .

and another . . .

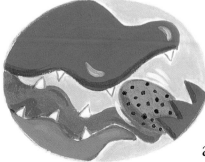

and another . . .

down to the very last cookie
(and every single crumb).

Yes—all of them were,
indeed,
deeeeeeeee-licious!

Then the kitchen door opened.

Mrs. Green was back.

She saw the crumbs on Mr. Green's chin.

She saw his bulging belly.

She saw the empty cookie sheet.

But she didn't see any cookies anywhere.

"I ate them ALL!"
Mr. Green confessed.
"Every one had snap,
crunch, *and* chew!
Yummmm . . .
deeeeeeeeee-licious!"

"Thank you!"
said Mrs. Green.
"I knew you would like them."

"Then *why,*"
asked Mr. Green,
"did you write this note?"

Mrs. Green took the note and opened it.

There were two pages, not one.

Mr. Green read the note again—*now* it made sense!

"You doubled the recipe?"

"Yes," said Mrs. Green, "you always ask for more,
so I used two times the ingredients—
and there are twice as many cookies."

She opened the refrigerator.
The second batch was ready to go.
"Shall we bake these now?"
she asked.

Mr. Green was not
listening—

$$20 \times 2 = 40$$
$$40 \times 2 = 80$$
$$80 \times 2 = 160$$
$$160 \times 2 = 320$$
$$320 \times 2 = 640$$
$$640 \times 2 = 1280$$
$$1280 \times 2 = 2560$$
$$2560 \times 2 = 5120$$

he was calculating cookies.

"What if we double the *doubled* recipe?" he asked.

"And then double that!

And double it again!

And again! And again! And again!

And . . ."

(He ran out of breath.)

"We would need more milk . . . ," said Mrs. Green,

"and a *much* bigger cookie jar."

48

Inventions

Mrs. Green put down her pencil.

She had been inventing all day long.

"What are you working on?" asked Mr. Green.

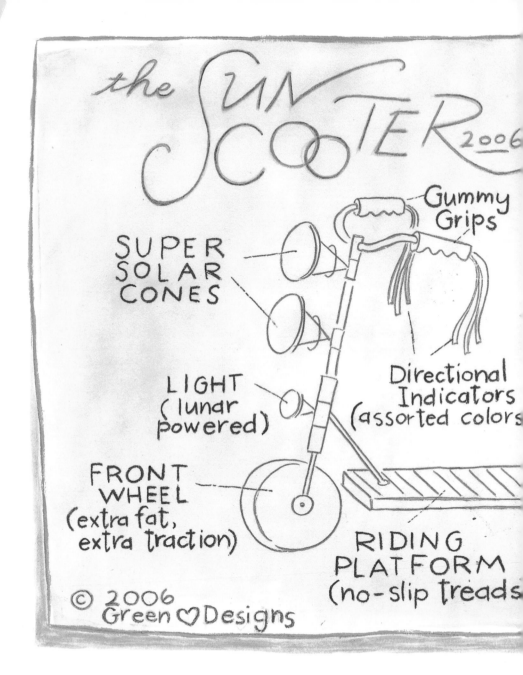

"A scooter," said Mrs. Green,

"a *solar-powered* scooter—

to go places I've never been before!"

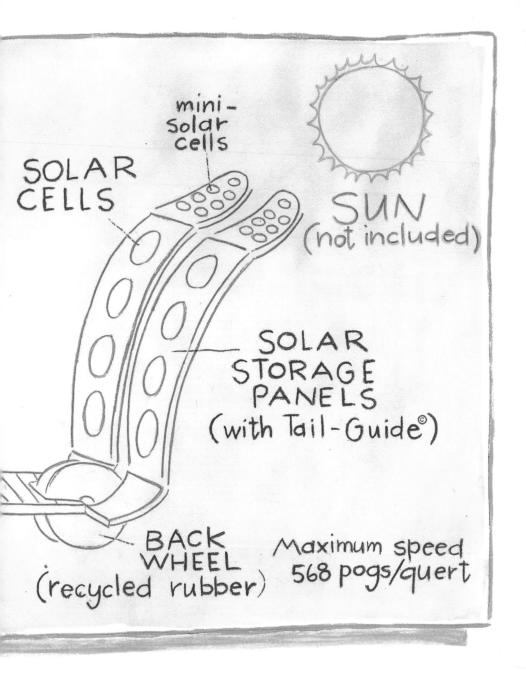

mini- solar cells

SOLAR CELLS

SUN
(not included)

SOLAR STORAGE PANELS
(with Tail-Guide©)

BACK WHEEL
(recycled rubber)

Maximum speed 568 pogs/quert

"May I come, too?" asked Mr. Green.

"Of course!" said Mrs. Green.

"I wouldn't go without you!"

"If *you* could invent anything," asked Mrs. Green,
"what would it be?"

"Anything?"
asked Mr. Green.
The wheels in his head
began to turn.
He thought about
some of his
favorite inventions.

Inventions like
airplanes . . .

eyeglasses . . .

telephones . . .

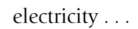

electricity . . .

and toasters, sliced bread, peanut butter—
not to mention Aunt Ernestene's Blue-ribbon
Raspberry Jam (from eastern Oregon)!

Mr. Green needed more time to think.

He also needed a snack.

"How about a slice of pie?"
he asked Mrs. Green.
"Pie *à la mode,* please,"
she said.
(Pie *à la mode* is French for
"pie with ice cream.")

Mrs. Green went back to work—
she still had lots to do.

Mr. Green went back
to thinking—
what could *he*
invent?

Then, suddenly, he got an idea.

"Thomas Alva Edison!" he shouted. "That's it!"

He ran out to their workshop.

Mr. Green worked all through the night.

He measured,

sawed,

drilled,

glued,

and hammered.

(He also yelled when
he hit his thumb.)

Mrs. Green worked all through the night, too.

She researched,

drew,

calculated,

erased,

and designed.

(She also whistled when
she sharpened her pencils.)

Mr. Green finished his invention at dawn.

He couldn't wait to show Mrs. Green—

and then the world!

"Introducing the *Green Machine 317*," he said.

"Please allow me to demonstrate."

"Take any pie . . .

put it inside . . .

select a setting . . .

pull the power lever
and . . . "

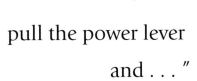

Ding, ding, ding!
"Six perfect slices—
no mess, no fuss,
noooooooo problem."

Mrs. Green was impressed,
but she had some questions.
"What if I need more slices,
smaller slices?"

"Easy as pie,"

said Mr. Green.

He grabbed another one.

"Simply adjust the dial,

pull the power lever, and . . . "

Ding, ding, ding!

"Eighteen perfect slices."

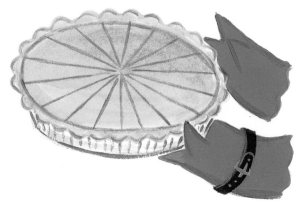

"Can it slice a cake, too?"

asked Mrs. Green.

"Certainly," said Mr. Green, "cakes, pizzas, and . . .

watermelon!"

His invention was easy, fast, and fun.

"But wait," said Mr. Green, "there's more!"

"Introducing the

À-la-mode-a-motor."

Mr. Green scooped ice cream

into the *À-la-mode-a-motor.*

He put a pie inside and

pulled the lever.

The *À-la-mode-a-motor*
jiggled and hummed,
rattled and shook,
sputtered and clunked,
then—
ding, ding, ding!—
it was done.

"Voilà!" said Mr. Green.
"Pie *à la mode*—especially for you."

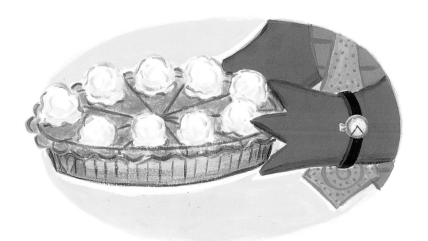

Mrs. Green was thrilled.
"The *Green Machine 317*
is an astonishing achievement—
we *must* take it with us!"

"Where are we going?"
asked Mr. Green.

"With my *Sun Scooters*," said Mrs. Green,

"we can go anywhere."

"*Anywhere* is just fine . . . ," said Mr. Green,

"as long as we go together!"